mnj

# I Used To Be the Baby

## BY ROBIN BALLARD

I Used To Be the Baby. Copyright © 2002 by Robin Ballard.
All rights reserved. Printed in Hong Kong by South China Printing Company (1988) Ltd. www.harperchildrens.com

Pen and ink and watercolors were used for the full-color art. The text type is Swiss 721 Light Bitstream.

Library of Congress Cataloging-in-Publication Data
Ballard, Robin. I used to be the baby / by Robin Ballard.   p.   cm.
"Greenwillow Books."   Summary: A young boy helps his mother take care of his baby brother.
ISBN 0-06-029586-4 (trade).   ISBN 0-06-029587-2 (lib. bdg.)   [1. Babies—Fiction. 2. Brothers—Fiction.]
I. Title.   PZ7.B2125 Iu 2002   [E]—dc21   2001023075
1 2 3 4 5 6 7 8 9 10 First Edition

GREENWILLOW BOOKS
*An Imprint of HarperCollinsPublishers*

For Susan Hirschman,
*who has helped me along my way*

I used to be the baby, but now I am big.

I have a baby brother, and I help Mommy take care of him.

He is hungry.

He needs his milk,
and I need mine.

He always wants to
take my toys.

I will give him some of his.

He is too little for TV.
He doesn't understand.

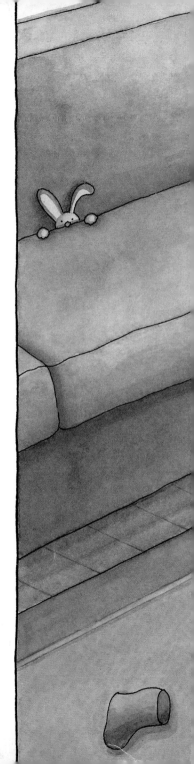

We could play
hide-and-go-seek.

It is nap time, and he is tired.

We are very quiet.

He doesn't like riding in the car.

I will sing him a song.

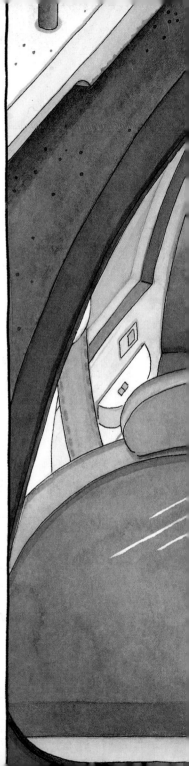

He is sad in the stroller.

I will hold his hand.

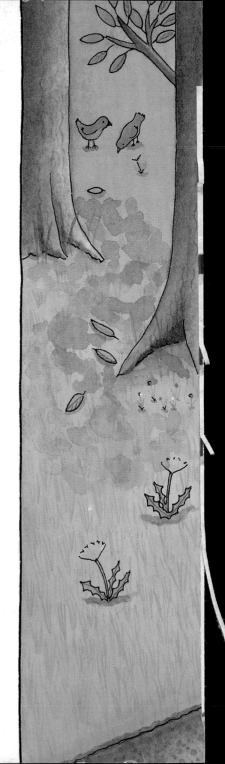

Sand can hurt your eyes.

He'll feel better on the swings.

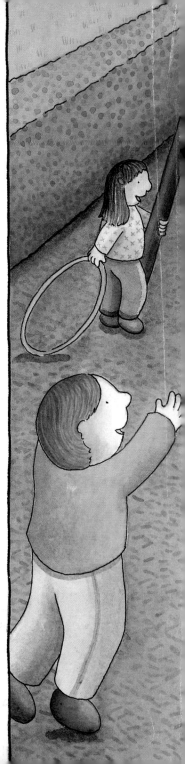

He doesn't like baths.

So I blow bubbles
for him to watch.

He tries to eat my books.

He can have his own books,
and I will read to him.

He doesn't like the dark.

I kiss him good-night.

I am the big brother.

But sometimes I like to be the baby too.